LUCY DANIELS

Little Animal Ark™

The Cheeky Chick

Illustrated by Andy Ellis

D0708539

Hodder
Children's
Books

A division of Hachette Children's Books

To George and Lucy

Special thanks to Linda Chapman

Little Animal Ark is a trademark of Working Partners Limited
Text copyright © 2002 Working Partners Limited
Created by Working Partners Limited, London, W6 0QT
Illustrations copyright © 2002 Andy Ellis

First published in Great Britain in 2002 by Hodder Children's Books

This edition published in 2007

The rights of Lucy Daniels and Andy Ellis to be identified as the author
and illustrator of this work respectively have been asserted by them in
accordance with the Copyright, Designs and Patents Act 1988.

5

A Catalogue record for this book is available from the
British Library

ISBN-13: 978 0 340 93257 5

Printed in Great Britain by
Clays Ltd, St Ives plc

Hodder Children's Books
A division of Hachette Children's Books
338 Euston Road, London NW1 3BH
An Hachette UK Company
www.hachette.co.uk

Chapter One

"How many hot cross buns are you going to make for the Easter festival, Gran?" Mandy Hope asked. She munched a biscuit as she watched her gran write a shopping list.

Grandma Hope put down her pen. "About two hundred," she said. "There are always lots of people at church for the Easter service."

"Can I help you make them?"
Mandy asked. She was staying at
her gran and grandad's for the
day. Her mum and dad were both
working. They were vets at
Animal Ark. Mandy wanted to be
a vet too when she grew up.

Her gran smiled. "I was
hoping you would," she said. "We
can start baking this afternoon
after we've been shopping."

While Grandma Hope finished
the list of what they needed,
Mandy looked at the cookery book.
Next to the recipe was a picture of
a baby rabbit, sniffing a huge pile
of hot cross buns.

Mandy grinned. "Look, it's

an Easter bunny, Gran," she said. Suddenly her eyes widened. She'd just had an idea. A really *great* idea!

"Gran!" she gasped. "We should have animals at the church on Sunday. They're part of Easter. They could come to the festival too."

Grandma Hope nodded. "You know, that sounds lovely, Mandy," she said.

"We could have baby rabbits and chicks – and lambs . . ." Mandy went on.

"Lambs might be a bit of a handful," Mandy's gran said with a smile. "But I'm sure everyone would love to have rabbits and chicks in the church. Why don't we go to the vicarage and ask Reverend Hadcroft?"

"Yes, let's!" Mandy cried, jumping to her feet.

Twenty minutes later, Mandy and her gran were sitting in Reverend

Hadcroft's living room.

"I think it's an excellent idea," Reverend Hadcroft said. "Do you think you can organise it, Mandy?"

"Oh yes," Mandy said. She looked at her gran. "Laura Baker's coming to the festival with her mum and dad. She might like to bring Nibbles, her rabbit. We could call in and ask her on the way home."

"Good idea," said Grandma Hope.

Reverend Hadcroft waved them off. "See you on Sunday!" he called.

"Bye!" Mandy called back. She skipped happily beside her gran.

"Bunnies and chicks! This is going to be the best Easter festival ever, Gran! Laura can bring Nibbles and . . ." Mandy had just thought of something else. "Gran!" she exclaimed. "Where are we going to find some chicks? My friends don't have hens!"

Grandma Hope patted Mandy's shoulder. "Why don't we sort out the rabbit first?" she said. "We can think about the chicks later."

Mandy nodded and they carried on towards Laura's house. But she still felt worried. Where were they going to get chicks from?

Chapter Two

"Hi, Laura," Mandy said, when
they arrived at the Bakers' house.
"I've come to ask if you'd like to
bring Nibbles to the Easter
festival on Sunday."

Laura's mouth fell open.
"Bring Nibbles to church?"
she said.

Mandy told Laura about
her bunnies and chicks idea.

"I'd love to bring Nibbles,"

said Laura, beaming happily.
She turned to her mum. "I can,
can't I, Mum?"

"I don't see why not." Mrs
Baker smiled.

Just then, Jill Redfern, one of Mandy's friends, came up the Bakers' path. Her mum was coming to have coffee with Mrs Baker, so Jill had come to play with Laura. "Hello, Mandy," she said. "What are you doing here?"

Mandy explained about bringing Nibbles to the Easter festival.

"What a brilliant idea!" said Jill. "I think Toto would love to come too." Then she sighed. "But tortoises aren't really Easter animals, are they?"

"No," Mandy agreed. "But that doesn't matter! You can bring Toto anyway. He's so lovely. I'm sure Reverend Hadcroft won't mind."

"Great!" said Jill. But then she looked sad again. "Oh, Toto hasn't woken up after his winter-time hibernation yet."

"Well, you can still help," Mandy said. "You could help me look after the chicks."

"I'd love to!" Jill cried.

Mandy looked at her gran. "If I can find some, of course," she said.

Mandy and Grandma Hope went to buy the bun ingredients. On the way out of the shop, Mandy saw a tall lady with grey hair waiting at the bus stop.

It was Kathy, one of her gran's friends. She

was carrying a small paper sack.

"Hello, Kathy," said Grandma Hope. "What's that you've got there?"

"Hello, Dorothy," said Kathy. She patted the paper sack. "It's a bag of chick crumbs."

"Chick crumbs?" Mandy said. "What are they?"

"I keep free-range hens," Kathy explained. "Some of them have had chicks. The chicks eat chick crumbs while they are little."

"Chicks!" Mandy gasped. She looked at her gran. "Gran! *Chicks!*"

Grandma Hope smiled and turned to her friend. "Kathy," she said. "We have a favour to ask."

As soon as Grandma Hope explained the problem, Kathy offered to bring some chicks for the Easter festival. "I've got some that are ten days old," she said. "They'll be just right."

"Oh, thank you!" Mandy said, beaming.

"Why don't you come round and have a look at them tomorrow, Mandy?" Kathy went on. "Your gran and I are meeting up to plan the flowers for the church. You could come with her."

"Yes please!" Mandy said. Suddenly she thought of something. "Would it be all right if my friend Jill comes as well?" she asked. "I told her she could help, you see."

"That's fine," Kathy said with a smile. "The more the merrier."

Chapter Three

Next morning, Grandma Hope drove Mandy and Jill to Kathy's house on the edge of Welford. At the back of the house was a small paddock with two wooden hen-houses and a large shed.

"Look at all the hens!" Mandy shouted, running over to the paddock with Jill.

There were hens everywhere – glossy brown ones, snowy white

ones and grey-and-white speckled
ones.

"Where are the chicks?"
Jill asked eagerly.

"In the shed," said Kathy.
"Come and see."

They followed her through
the gate and into the small
wooden building.

"Oh, wow!" Mandy gasped.

Right in front of her was a
pen with the sweetest chicks that
she had ever seen. They pecked
around in the shavings on the
floor of the pen. Their yellow and
brown feathers were fluffy and
their dark eyes were bright.

"They're adorable!" said Grandma Hope.

Kathy picked up two chicks. "This one is Cara," she said, handing one to Jill.

"And this one is Charlie," she said, handing the other to Mandy.

"How can you tell them apart?" Mandy asked. The chicks looked identical to her!

"They each have slightly different markings," Kathy explained. "There are ten chicks altogether, and they all look a little bit different. Look carefully and you'll see that Cara's got a pale tummy. Charlie's got a black patch on the top of his head."

"Oh yes," Mandy said, looking down at Charlie. He put his head on one side and cheeped loudly at her. Then he pecked at her hand.

Mandy laughed. His beak was only tiny and it didn't hurt.

Charlie looked up at her and cheeped as if he was laughing too.

"Charlie's the liveliest," Kathy told her. "He's always trying to explore." She picked up a basket next to the chicks' pen. "I thought you could put the chicks in this for the festival."

Mandy looked at the basket. It seemed just right.

"We'll fill it with clean straw, and I'll find some ribbons to decorate it," Kathy said.

"That's great! Thank you, Kathy," said Mandy.

"The chicks are going to look lovely!" said Jill.

"Yes, it's very kind of you to go to all this trouble, Kathy," said Grandma Hope.

Kathy smiled, then turned to Mandy and Jill. "Now, while we go and talk about the flowers, why don't you two see if you can get the chicks used to sitting in the basket?" she said.

She took a paper bag off the window ledge and handed it to Mandy. "Here are some chick crumbs. You can use them to get the chicks to sit still. The straw's over there," she added, pointing to a heap in the corner. "OK?"

"OK!" Mandy and Jill said happily.

After Kathy and Grandma Hope had left, Mandy and Jill put Cara and Charlie back into the pen. Then they filled the basket with a bed of straw.

"Let's put the chicks in now," Mandy said.

Jill frowned. "I thought Kathy said there were ten of them."

"She did," Mandy said.

"Well, I can only count nine," said Jill.

Mandy stared. Jill was right. There were only nine chicks! One of the chicks had disappeared!

Mandy looked closely at the remaining chicks. Not one of them had a black mark on their head. "It's Charlie!" she said. "He's gone!"

Chapter Four

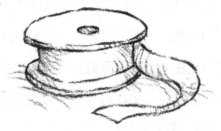

"We'd better tell Kathy that
Charlie is missing," said Jill,
sounding alarmed.

But suddenly Mandy's sharp
eyes noticed a bit of straw at the
bottom of the pile in the corner.
It was moving.

"Look!" she said, grabbing
Jill's arm.

The straw moved again.
Then she heard a loud *"Cheep!"*

Suddenly Charlie's yellow and black head popped out.

"Oh, Charlie!" Mandy said, hurrying over and picking him up. "What are you doing over there?"

He cheeped happily at her.

"I wonder how he got out," said Jill.

Mandy looked into the pen. The water container had been knocked over. "I bet he climbed on that and hopped out," she said.

She put Charlie back into the pen. He ran straight over to the container and hopped on top. It was easy to see how he had escaped!

Jill refilled the container and put it back into the pen the right way up. Then they put Charlie and the other chicks into the Easter basket. The chicks ran to the sides and began to hop up and down as if they were trying to get out.

"They don't look very happy," Mandy said, feeling worried.

"Let's put the chick crumbs in," said Jill.

Mandy fetched the bag and put a handful of chick crumbs into the basket. They looked like stale breadcrumbs. But the chicks seemed to like them. They stopped trying to get out and began to peck in the straw.

All except Charlie. He stayed at the side of the basket, pulling at a loose piece of basket with his beak.

"I think Charlie's trying to escape again!" Mandy grinned.

Just then the shed door opened and Kathy and Grandma Hope came in. Grandma Hope was carrying a paper bag. Kathy held a tray with two glasses of juice and a plate of chocolate biscuits. "We thought you might like a snack," she said.

"And Kathy's found some ribbon for you to decorate the basket with," Grandma Hope added, holding out the bag.

"Oh, wow!" Mandy said. She opened the bag and pulled out a roll of green ribbon. "Look at these, Jill!"

It didn't take them long to tie on the ribbon. Soon, the handle was covered in colourful bows.

"Now it really *does* look like an Easter basket," said Jill.

"It looks lovely!" Grandma Hope said. "And aren't the chicks being good?"

Just then, the biggest bow started to come undone. Charlie was standing at the side of the basket, pulling at one end of the ribbon! He looked very pleased with himself.

They all burst out laughing.

"Oh, Charlie," Mandy said, picking him up and cuddling him. "You really are a very cheeky chick!"

Charlie looked at her and opened his beak. *"Cheep!"* he agreed.

Chapter Five

Mandy was so keen to get to the church the next morning that she almost dragged her mum and dad out of the house. "We've got to hurry," she said.

"It's only ten-thirty, Mandy," said Mrs Hope, locking the front door. "The service doesn't start for half an hour."

"I know, but I've got to meet Kathy," Mandy said.

"And Jill and Laura and Gran."

Mandy's dad took a deep breath and sang a few notes. He was going to be singing in the church choir.

"Come on, Dad!" Mandy said. She led the way out of the drive and along the lane to the church.

The sun was shining and every garden they passed was filled with bright yellow daffodils. But Mandy hardly noticed. She couldn't wait to see Laura's rabbit, Nibbles, and all the chicks!

Grandma Hope and Kathy were at the church arranging flowers when Mandy and her mum and dad arrived.

"The chicks are in a box under the display table," Kathy said to Mandy. "I thought it best not to put them in their basket until you were here to keep an eye on them."

Mandy hurried over to the display table. Her gran's hot cross buns were piled up on enormous white plates. There was a large chocolate chick wrapped in gold foil. Someone had brought a bowl of pretty painted eggs. And right in the middle of the table was the chicks' Easter basket with its green ribbons. It all looked lovely!

Just then, Laura arrived with Nibbles. His black-and-white fur was clean and smooth, and he had a smart blue bow round his neck. But where was Jill?

Mandy stroked Nibbles's soft ears as she watched people start to arrive.

"I can't wait for Jill any longer," she said. "I'd better put the chicks into their basket."

She opened the cardboard
box under the table and lifted out
the chicks one by one. As soon as
she put Charlie into the basket,
he went straight over to a bow
and pecked at it.

"Don't peck that, silly,"
Mandy said, scattering in some
chick crumbs. "Peck these."

Laura gave
Nibbles a dried
apple ring to eat.
"Mum's got his
plastic carrying
box," she told
Mandy. "We're
going to put him
in that during
the service. I've
put some more
apple pieces in
there for him."

"Mandy! Laura!"

Mandy and Laura looked
round. Jill was hurrying towards
them and in her arms she was
holding . . .

"Toto!" Mandy gasped.

"He woke up this morning," Jill explained. She pointed to a purple ribbon she had tied around her pet's shell. "I've tried to make him look as Eastery as I can. That's why I'm late."

Mandy grinned. "He looks great!" she said.

"And so does the table," said Jill. She gave Toto a cabbage leaf to munch on.

"It certainly does," said Mandy's grandad. He came over to admire the display more closely. "It looks a real picture!" he added.

Soon there was a whole crowd of people gathered round them. Everyone seemed really pleased to see Nibbles and Toto and the chicks at the Easter festival.

"Well done, girls!" said Reverend Hadcroft. He beamed at Mandy, Jill and Laura.

They grinned back happily.

It was time for the service to start. Laura and Jill took their pets and joined their families. Mandy squeezed in beside her mum in the pew nearest to the display table.

Reverend Hadcroft began. "Welcome to our Easter festival. Let's start by singing our first hymn,

All Things Bright and Beautiful."

As everyone stood up, Mandy glanced across at the chick basket. The chicks were still pecking happily in the straw. *One, two, three, four, five,* Mandy counted in her head, *six, seven, eight, nine* . . . She stopped. Nine!

There couldn't just be nine chicks. Maybe she'd made a mistake.

She counted again as fast as she could. But, no – one of the chicks was missing! Her eyes darted over the fluffy yellow heads. Where was Charlie?

Chapter Six

Mandy slipped out of the pew
and crept over to the display
table. Her heart was pounding.
If Charlie escaped out of the
church he would be in real
danger.

But there was no sign of the
cheeky little chick.

Then Mandy spotted a
trail of tiny yellow feathers on
the table . . .

It led to a plate of hot cross buns. Mandy's eyes widened. One of the buns looked a bit nibbled. Nibbled by a chick!

Charlie had definitely been there. But where was he now?

"*Cheep!*"

Mandy held her breath. The sound had come from behind the hot cross buns.

Very carefully, Mandy moved the plate . . .

And saw Charlie, standing beside the big chocolate chick, with his head on one side.

"*Cheep!*" he said, as if he was talking to it.

Mandy burst out laughing – just as the hymn ended. Everyone turned to stare at her.

Mandy's hand flew to her mouth.

"Mandy!" her mum exclaimed. "*What* are you doing?"

Bright red, Mandy said, "Sorry, Mum. It's Charlie, he escaped . . ." She pointed to the table.

"Cheep! Cheepity cheep!"

Mrs Hope looked amazed as Charlie pecked happily at the chocolate chick.

"Cheep!" he said again.

"Oh dear," said Mrs Hope. But Mandy could see her mum was smiling.

Other people nearby saw what Charlie was doing. They began to laugh and point. Soon everyone in the church was laughing, as they watched the little chick cheeping away to his chocolate friend.

Mandy looked at Reverend Hadcroft. To her relief, she saw that he was laughing too. He came over to the table, and reached out towards Charlie. "Come here, little fella," he said. "Let's put you back in your basket."

But as soon as Charlie saw the Reverend's hands coming, he ran down the table and hid behind a pile of painted eggs.

"See if he'll come out for some chick crumbs, Mandy," said Mrs Hope.

Mandy got the bag of chick crumbs from under the table and took out a handful. "Here, Charlie," she said.

Charlie peeped out. He looked at the chick crumbs and then cheeped as if to say, *"No, thank you!"* Then he ran to the other end of the table.

"Quick, Mandy!" said Mrs Hope. "Stop him!"

Mandy thought fast. What she needed was something Charlie *really* liked. Her eyes fell on Charlie's nibbled bun.

She grabbed it, broke a bit off and held it out. "Come on, Charlie," she called softly.

Charlie stared at the hot cross bun.

Mandy's heart beat faster. "Here you are, boy," she breathed. "Yummy hot cross bun."

Charlie put his head on one side as if he was thinking hard. Then he hopped over and pecked at the piece of bun. The next second he was safe in Mandy's hands.

Mandy heard everyone let out a sigh of relief.

"Good thinking, Mandy," said Reverend Hadcroft.

Mandy stroked the top of Charlie's head. "Let's put you back where you belong," she said.

She carefully put Charlie back in the basket with the other chicks. He cheeped crossly and flapped his tiny wings.

Mandy gave him another chunk of hot cross bun. "Now you just stay there and be quiet," she whispered to him.

Charlie pecked at the hot cross bun. *"Cheep!"* he said happily, as if to say, *"OK!"*

At the end of the service, Reverend Hadcroft smiled round at everyone. "So that's the end of our Easter service," he said. "I'd like to thank all those people who have helped to organise things. In particular, our young animal handlers, Mandy Hope, Laura Baker and Jill Redfern. The festival just wouldn't have been the same without them." He began to clap.

As everyone in the church joined in, Mandy felt her cheeks go bright red.

Mandy's mum squeezed her hand. "Well done, love," she whispered, sounding very proud.

"Now, there are hot cross buns on the display table," said Reverend Hadcroft. His eyes twinkled. "Providing Charlie the chick has left us some, of course!"

Laughing, people began to head for the display.

"Would you like a hot cross bun, love?" asked Mrs Hope.

"Yes, please," Mandy said. She went to check on the chicks. Charlie was still pecking at his bun. Mandy lifted him out and stroked his soft head.

Reverend Hadcroft came up to her. "Happy Easter, Mandy," he said. He smiled down at Charlie. "And Happy Easter to you too,

Charlie," he added. "You've certainly made this a festival to remember!"

Then he leaned over and lifted the chocolate chick from the display. "This is for you, Mandy," he said. "You can share it with Jill and Laura. You deserve it after all your hard work."

"Thank you!" Mandy said, delighted.

Charlie looked up at Reverend Hadcroft from Mandy's hand. A crumb was hanging from his beak. *"Cheep!"* he said cheekily. *"Cheepity cheepity cheep!"*

Chapter One

"Dad, is it time for my surprise now?" Mandy Hope asked eagerly. She finished her apple pie and custard, and put down her spoon. "I've been waiting for ages!"

Mr Hope laughed. "Just let me finish my pudding, Mandy!" he said.

"Mandy's going to burst if she doesn't find out what the surprise is soon," Mrs Hope said with a smile.

"I'm so full, I think I *might* burst!" Mandy joked, patting her tummy. "That was a lovely lunch. Thanks, Gran."

Mandy and her mum and dad were having Sunday lunch with Gran and Grandad Hope. On the way to Lilac Cottage, Mr Hope had told Mandy that he had a surprise for her. She couldn't wait to find out what it was. All she knew was that they would have to go in the Land-rover.

Mandy hoped it was something to do with animals. Mandy *loved* animals! Her mum and dad were vets at Animal Ark, and Mandy wanted to be a vet too one day.

"Anyone for seconds?" her gran asked. She picked up the jug of custard.

"Not for me, thanks," Mr Hope said. "I'd better not keep Mandy waiting any longer!"

"Don't worry," said Mandy's grandad. "I'll finish up the rest of the apple pie!"

Mandy dashed into the hall to get her coat. She wondered where her dad was taking her.

"I'm ready, Dad," she said, rushing back into the living-room. Just then, she spotted her gran's knitting bag and remembered something important. "I've got something to ask Gran," she said.

"What's that?" Gran smiled.

"We're doing a project at school," Mandy said. "And tomorrow we're looking at all the things we can do with wool."